Grandpa's Music
A Story About Alzheimer's

by Alison Acheson
Illustrated by Bill Farnsworth

Albert Whitman & Company, Morton Grove, Illinois

To all the Home Teams.
Especially the team of Jeanne, Elyse, Cassidy, and Nolan.
—AA—

For Maurice.
—BF—

Library of Congress Cataloging-in-Publication Data

Acheson, Alison, 1964-
Grandpa's music : a story about Alzheimer's / by Alison Acheson ;
illustrated by Bill Farnsworth.
p. cm.
Summary: Although Alzheimer's disease makes it difficult for Callie's grandfather
to remember things, his family keeps him occupied, and Callie's special
task is to help him enjoy playing the piano and singing favorite songs.
ISBN 978-0-8075-3052-8
[1. Alzheimer's disease—Fiction. 2. Grandfathers—Fiction. 3. Family life—Fiction.]
I. Farnsworth, Bill, ill. II. Title.
PZ7.A176Grd 2009   [E]—dc22   2008055792

Text copyright © 2009 by Alison Acheson.
Illustrations copyright © 2009 by Bill Farnsworth.
Published in 2009 by Albert Whitman & Company,
6340 Oakton Street, Morton Grove, Illinois 60053-2723.
Printed in China.
10 9 8 7 6 5 4 3 2 1

The design is by Lindaanne Donohoe.

For more information about Albert Whitman & Company,
visit our web site at www.albertwhitman.com.

*M*emories can be rich and wonderful. But the memory loss that comes with Alzheimer's can be frustrating, not only for people with the disease, but for their loved ones as well.

When I began to write *Grandpa's Music*, I listened to families and caregivers of people with Alzheimer's. Their favorite experiences included story-telling, often venturing into make-believe. Rather than dwelling on the past or the future, they tried to focus on the moment, sometimes in playful and imaginative ways.

It's good to share stories, art, and music with people affected by Alzheimer's. Especially music—research has shown that we all remember songs from our early to mid-teens the best. This music stays with people, even while Alzheimer's or other diseases of the brain cause them to lose many other memories and knowledge. Often, the ability to play a musical instrument will remain even into the later stages of Alzheimer's.

Humans learn with all parts of their selves, not just their minds. We learn with our bodies and our senses. Grandpa in *Grandpa's Music* plays the piano by relying on "muscle memory" in his fingers. People with Alzheimer's often remember—with their feet—how to dance, especially to a favorite song! It's not easy having a family member with Alzheimer's, but embracing creativity can bring surprises and unexpected pleasures.

I wish you many memories, old and new, and stories and songs.

—Alison Acheson

It's time," says Dad.

Time for Grandpa to move into our home.

He does, with his songbooks and his little cat, Baby Ruth.

Grandpa goes to bed early that first night.

"All of us need to help make this work for Grandpa," Dad says. "I'm going to cook dinner every night."

"And I've made up a routine for Grandpa's day," says Mom. "That way Grandpa will know what step comes next."

Dad looks at Joel. "Grandpa is going to give you his car." He writes on the board under Joel's name: DRIVE GRANDPA TO DOCTOR'S OFFICE. TO PARK. TO SENIORS' CENTER.

"What about you, Callie?" asks Mom.

"We can play catch, and I can help Grandpa remember his hat," I say. Grandpa never goes anywhere without it.

It's settled, then.

Or it is until morning.

"What do I do?" asks Grandpa.

"We're taking care of you, Grandpa," I tell him.

There's a look on Grandpa's face I've never seen before.

So I write GRANDPA on the board, and think of all the things he's good at.

TAKE CARE OF GARDEN.
PEEL POTATOES.
KNEAD BREAD.

Then I see him holding the sheet music. MAKE MUSIC, I write.

A smile spreads over his face.

After breakfast, he goes right to the
piano and begins to play. He sings, too.

It's early spring, and he spends a lot of time watering the garden, turning compost, and planting.

In the afternoon, Grandpa kneads the bread dough—*thump, thump* on the counter. He helps with dinner. He peels carrots and potatoes. Sometimes he makes the salad. Dad reminds him how to wash mushrooms.

Sometimes we watch a ball game. And every evening before bedtime, he plays the piano.

One day, at the end
of summer, I find him
out in the garden. The
hose has been running
a long time. I get a towel
for his feet.

At dinnertime, Grandpa says, "I can make the lettuce," and after dinner he sits at the piano and plays "You Are My Sunshine" and "Take Me Out to the Ball Game." Sometimes Grandpa forgets the words to the sunshine song, but he remembers "Take Me Out." It reminds me of the times we've gone to Wrigley Field, Grandpa and me.

Next morning, I find him at the chalkboard.
"I need to find the piano, Callie," Grandpa says.
But he heads down the hall in the other direction.
"This way, Grandpa," I say.

On New Year's Eve, Grandpa hurts his hand
with the vegetable peeler. Dad bandages it. But
at midnight, he can still play "Auld Lang Syne."

It's springtime again, and a night
when the moon is full. I can hear piano
music and I follow the sound.
Grandpa's fingers don't need the
light to remember the notes. Most of
the time, his fingers remember.

I wonder what parts of me remember. Maybe my nose. I'll always remember how Grandpa smells—a bit like garden soil, and a bit like the kitchen and the bread he makes.

Tonight he can't remember all the words to the song he's playing.

I start to sing: "Take me out to the ball game, take me out with the crowd..."

In the moonlight, I see his face. He looks worried.

"We can make up the words, Grandpa," I tell him. I start to sing again: "Come with me to the ball game…"

He grins. "…We'll hit out to the moon…"

I sing: "Then we can sail from third to home…"

And Grandpa breaks in. "We'll make up words 'til the cows start to roam!"

We laugh, then sing together: "Root, root, root for the home team!" and Grandpa gives me a hug.

"It's time," says Mom.

Time for Grandpa to live in a place with doctors and nurses.

The place is nearby. We'll be able to visit. I hug Baby Ruth before we leave the house. She knows, too, I think.

As we set off, I know nothing is going to be the same.

The place is green on the outside. Inside people are sitting, some playing cards, some asleep in chairs, a few working on a puzzle. A nurse shows us around.

We see Grandpa's room, and the
dining room. There's the common room,
and Grandpa sees something familiar.

It's a piano. He sits and stares at the keys.

He begins to hum, and I sit beside him.

"We can make up words," I tell him.

He plays a few notes.

"What about the home team?" asks Grandpa.

"The song says, 'If they don't win it's a shame,'" I remind him.

Grandpa shakes his head. "I've never liked that part. But I sure like going to the game—maybe we can sing about that."

"Yes," I tell him. "We can always
sing about that."